## Dedication

This book is dedicated to all the loving
foster families for rescue dogs.

Thank you for saving these furry blessings,
until they reach their Forever Homes.

*Alli,
you are unique in
so many ways!
— M. Wayne Adam*

# Introduction

Dear Readers and Listeners,

*Teddy Tales* follows the adventures of a real rescue dog who is welcomed into a family and neighborhood. In each chapter, Teddy explores some of the same adventures and problems that face preschool and elementary-age children, such as: making friends, starting school, haircuts, fears, making bad choices, going on vacation, and feeling accepted. Along the way, children will also learn about pet care. The stories provide children and their caregivers, teachers, and counselors with opportunities for important talks about life.

Teddy, the rescue puppy, would like to meet you. He would run up to you, give a little jump, and then deliver some puppy kisses. Then he might lie down and let you rub his belly before running to bring you his favorite toy. The two of you could play fetch until Teddy gets tired and needs a drink of water. If you are feeling quiet and just want to read a book, he would lie at your feet, perhaps with his head on your foot. If he smelled peanut butter, he would wake up and run to the kitchen for a treat. Later, he would love to take a walk with you in the woods and chase squirrels or rabbits. Most of all, Teddy would like to become your "guide dog" or "therapy dog," while you read his stories.

# Teddy Tales

### The Adventures of a Rescue Puppy and His Friends

## Karen Spruill

ILLUSTRATIONS BY MARK WAYNE ADAMS

Text and illustrations copyright © 2011 by Karen Spruill.
The Teddy Tales imprints and characters are a
Karen Spruill Books trademark.
All rights reserved.

No part of this publication may be reproduced or transmitted
in any form or by any means, electronic or mechanical,
including photocopying, recording, or by any information
storage and retrieval system, now known or to be invented,
without permission in writing from Karen Spruill Books.

For information regarding permissions,
contact Karen Spruill Books at:

Karen Spruill Books
P. O. Box 782363
Orlando, FL 32878-2363
www.karenspruill.com

Written by Karen Spruill
Illustrations by Mark W. Adams
Editing by Page One Communications
Printing by Lightning Source

Karen Spruill
First Edition

ISBN-13: 978-0-9836723-0-2

First Printing 2011
Published in the United States of America
Printed in the United States of America

# Table of Contents

Teddy—the Rescue Puppy .................................... 1

"Teddy—What Kind of Dog is That?" ..................... 9

Teddy and the Tummy Ache ................................ 17

Teddy Goes to School ........................................ 23

Teddy's Terrible Teeth ....................................... 29

Teddy Makes Friends ........................................ 35

Teddy's Big Sleepover ....................................... 43

Teddy—Curious and Cautious ............................ 49

Teddy and the Haircut ....................................... 55

Teddy the Runaway .......................................... 63

Teddy's Beach Vacation ..................................... 69

Teddy's Dog Family .......................................... 75

# Teddy—the Rescue Puppy

*Your past doesn't really matter as much as who you are now
—and what you can become!*

Once there was a dog named Queenie, whose family moved away and left her all alone at home. Queenie missed her people, but she especially missed her food and water.

After a few days, some of the neighbors could hear Queenie crying inside the building. One of them decided to call the special police who try to protect animals. The officers were able to open the door where Queenie lived, "Here, Girl—Good Girl," they said, and they took her outside for food and water.

The officers noticed that Queenie looked as if she were going to have puppies soon. So they took her to the county shelter for animals without homes or owners. Soon, Queenie had her babies, and there were nine little puppies crowded into her kennel room.

One day, some kind women from Buddies for Life came to the shelter and decided to rescue Queenie and her puppies so that they could quickly find forever homes for the family. These women had lots of dogs at their foster homes. They worked hard to put ads in the papers and pictures of the puppies on the Internet, so they could find good homes.

Across town, Kay was very sad. Her dog had gotten sick and died. Her children were grown up, and the house seemed empty and quiet without a dog inside. The neighbors noticed that Kay was going on her walks alone, and sometimes they would stop and ask, "What happened to your dog?" Then Kay would tell them the sad story about her dog, and she would feel even more alone on her walks.

One night, Kay's next-door neighbor Jen knocked on the door and asked if Kay would let Josh, her 7-year-old son, stay with Kay after school on two afternoons each week. Kay said, "Yes, I think I have room for a boy." Then Kay started making some cookies before Josh's first visit.

But a boy is not a dog, and a dog is not a boy. Kay still missed having a dog. So she decided that she and her husband, Sam, needed to get another dog to share their home. She started looking at ads in the newspapers and on the computer.

Kay wanted a dog that would be: not too little and not too big; not too loud, not too shy; not too much energy, and not too much fur. Yet she knew that it really didn't matter if the dog was a boy or girl or whether or not her new dog had a fancy title. She just wanted a healthy, happy, dog that would grow up to be a good friend. Many of the people who sold dogs wanted lots of money for their dogs. Some of the sellers also had lots of rules about how to own a dog or when people could visit their dogs, and many of them lived far away.

Kay felt sad again. She didn't know how she would find just the right dog. She wished that someone could bring her a nice puppy.

Then one day, she looked on her computer and saw a picture of the cutest little puppy—one of Queenie's puppies!

"Oh, that puppy needs a home, and he is right here in my city," said Kay.

Kay filled out an application so she could adopt a dog, and she sent a message to the kind people at Buddies for Life. Debbie answered the message and told Kay that she could bring the puppy to her house so she could meet him. They could come next Wednesday!

On the following Wednesday, Kay was very excited about meeting the puppy. She wondered how old he would be when she saw him. What if he turned out to be a big, almost-grown-up puppy? What if he were scared, or cried, or barked a lot? Right on time, Debbie and the puppy arrived at her front door. The puppy was inside a pet carrying crate, and Debbie let him out to meet Kay. He was only eight weeks old, but he wagged his tail and walked right up to Kay. He started exploring and seemed very happy to be at her house.

"Oh, he's so cute," Kay said, bending down. "He looks like a little Teddy Bear."

They walked around her back yard, and Kay asked Debbie about what had happened to the puppy's family. In no time at all, Kay was sure that she wanted to keep the puppy. She loved his cute little face, fat little tummy, happy little tail, and bright sassy eyes. She hoped that someday, he could be a therapy dog to help her visit special people who need extra love. This puppy was just right—he was not expensive, he was healthy, and most of all, he needed a home.

However, someone else was interested in the puppy so Kay had to decide that day! Since she did not want to lose this puppy, she told Debbie, "Yes, I want to adopt him." Debbie seemed very glad that the puppy would have a nice home, even though she would miss him.

Kay signed an agreement to take good care of the puppy, and then she paid Debbie some money so that Buddies for Life could rescue more dogs. After Debbie said good-bye to the puppy, Kay took him to visit her veterinarian. Everyone at the veterinarian's office thought the puppy was very cute. He got a shot and some treats. But he didn't have a name yet, so they wrote "Puppy" on his new record.

Then Kay took him to the pet store to buy food, a crate, a bed, some bowls, and some toys. The puppy was very excited to visit the store and see all the rows of food, toys, and people. He got so tired that while Kay shopped, the puppy fell asleep on her shoulder. When she paid for her purchases, a man noticed the puppy and said he was cute. Then he asked, "What is his name?"

"I don't know," Kay answered, "I just got him."

That evening, Sam met the puppy, and they had fun playing for a while.

"What are we going to name him?" he asked Kay.

"I don't know yet. I'm thinking," she replied. His name had to be just right—a name that wasn't too fancy, too plain, too hard to say, or too silly to call out in the neighborhood.

# Teddy Tales

At bedtime, the puppy had his own bedroom kennel, with a special dog bed and some stuffed toys. He cried a little in the night when he needed to go outside, and he missed having warm dog bodies next to him.

The very next day, Josh came to Kay's house and met the puppy. Josh giggled and giggled when the puppy licked his face and squirmed all over him. Josh and Kay and the puppy started going on walks, playing with toys, and getting to know each other. Soon, the puppy loved his new home.

When Kay and the puppy went on their walks, some of the neighborhood children met him and asked, "What is his name?" Kay wasn't sure. She wanted to give him just the right name. Each day, Sam or one of their children would call Kay on the phone and ask, "What have you named the puppy?" Even Debbie wrote to Kay and asked about his new name.

Kay thought and thought about a name. She thought of black, playful, and boy dog names: Shadow, Dusty, Sparky, Coal, Scruffy, Spunky, and Rascal. She woke up at night and thought of names. Then she wrote a long list. Kay thought that he could be an Ewok, like those of the Star Wars movies. Sam suggested that since the puppy wanted to chew everything, he could be Chewie, after the Chewbacca character. Josh said, "He should be Devil, since he bites my shoes," but Kay said, "No." Kay knew that the puppy's name had to be a lovable, happy name—just like him.

After several days of trying to find the perfect name, Kay went to the pet store to get a name tag for his collar, and she had made her decision—his name would be Teddy, because he really did look like a huggable little Teddy Bear. Finally, he had a name, and he was an official part of the family.

Now when Teddy takes walks around the neighborhood, some of the children greet him with, "Hi, Teddy!" and he hears his name and starts to wag his tail.

He's Teddy, the rescue puppy. Kay rescued him so that he could have a forever home. And Teddy rescued Kay and Sam's quiet, empty house with his happy, playful puppiness.

# Teddy's Talking Time Questions for People

1. *What are some supplies that you might need when bringing home a new dog?*

2. *Who gets rescued when pets have a Forever Home?*

   **Write your answers below.**

## "Teddy—What Kind of Dog Is That?"

*Everyone needs to be loved for who they are*

Kay likes to watch dog shows on television. Many kinds of dogs, from countries all over the world, compete to be the best dog. All of the dogs in the shows are "pedigreed"—they come from dog families where everyone is supposed to look and act a certain way.

Kay has owned many dogs in her life. When her children were young, the family owned a Scottish Terrier with short legs and perky ears. Later, her daughter helped to pick out a St. Bernard puppy that grew and grew until she weighed as much as Kay. After that, they owned a Labrador Retriever that loved to fetch toys and get into the garbage cans. All of those puppies had come with special papers that were "registered" to prove that they were the kind of dogs that people called them.

Almost as soon as Kay found Teddy, her new puppy, people started asking her, "What kind of dog is that?" Teddy was black, with dark eyes, sharp teeth, floppy little ears, a fuzzy face, and a long tail. He looked like lots of dogs but not really like any kind of dog. Kay had seen a picture of his mother dog and a few of his brothers and sisters, but he had a mysterious father dog. No one knew what that dog was or what he looked like. Teddy's picture on the Internet had been labeled, "Lab/terrier/spaniel." Sometimes Kay joked and called him an Irish Spanrador Terrier.

When Kay took Teddy to the veterinarian for his vaccinations, she asked the doctor, "How big do you think he will grow?" The vet checked Teddy over and said that he couldn't be sure, but that whatever Teddy weighed at four months old, you could probably double that amount for what he would weigh as a grown-up dog.

When Kay started walking Teddy around the neighborhood, people stopped to ask her, "What kind of dog is that?" And she didn't know. Sometimes she told them what Teddy's mother had looked like and how big she was. Often, Kay would just say, "I don't know," or "mixed breed." At least she could tell them his name. Sometimes, she would just say, "He's a rescue puppy." And sometimes, a person would reply, "They are the best kind!"

Once, when they were walking with Kay's daughter, Lilly, and her dog, a neighbor said, "Oh, pretty," to Lilly's dog. Kay felt a little sad, because Teddy really wasn't pretty yet, but he was very cute and smart. Then the woman looked at Teddy and added, "Oh, you're pretty too." On another walk, Kay saw a person look at Teddy and laugh. Another neighbor said, "He sort of looks like a Scottie dog." And someone else said that "maybe a Wheaten Terrier" was his father. Once, a neighbor said, "Oh, yeah. I used to have a mutt," as he scratched Teddy's ears. Kay did not like Teddy being called a mutt. That word made her think of some kind of dog that no one loved or that would live in a junk yard chained to a post!

When she told Sam about some of the things that people said about the way Teddy looked, he said that she should call Teddy "an Irish Lizard Hound," since he liked to chase the little lizards in their yard. Kay laughed. She just knew that Teddy was very special.

After Teddy lived with Kay and Sam a few weeks, he started to grow. He ate lots of his puppy food and drank lots of water. He could reach things on top of the coffee table. He could see the blanket on top of the couch cushion. He could reach lots of flowers in the garden. His legs and tail got longer. As he grew, he found lots of ways to get into trouble! Every time that Josh, the neighbor boy, stayed after school at their house, he would say, "Teddy is getting bigger." But the part of Teddy that people noticed right away was his fuzzy face. When he was little, he had a white spot on his chin and one on his chest. As a bigger puppy, he had a white ring around his nose and mouth and light circles around his eyes. His legs started to turn gray, and the fur under his outer coat was turning gray also.

Teddy really didn't look like most of the dogs in the neighborhood. Sam and Kay took pictures of him to send to their family and friends so that they could enjoy his special looks. Kay wished that they could come meet him and see what a great dog he was becoming. Kay really thought that Teddy ought to be in television commercials or movies so that lots of people could enjoy him.

When Kay and Sam's daughter, Lilly, received her pictures of Teddy, she called, and they talked about different kinds of dogs. "I wish I knew what his daddy dog looked like," said Kay. "I looked in my dog book, but Teddy just doesn't look like any of them."

"Well, I think he fits into our family just right," laughed Lilly. "Our family is German, Scottish, English, and Native American.

Now you have a son-in-law who is Chinese, and a daughter-in-law who is Bolivian, Italian, and Greek. Teddy is just like the rest of us!"

One day when Kay and Josh took Teddy outside for a walk around the neighborhood, they met some of the neighbors. Then one of the children's mothers noticed Teddy and said, "Oh, he's getting so big. And look at that face!" Several children ran up to Teddy calling his name, "Teddy!" Julian and Katie asked, "Can we pet him?" and Kay said, "Thank you for asking for permission to pet him. Just be careful of his sharp teeth."

Then Julian said, "I will miss Teddy."

Kay asked him, "Are you going away?"

Julian's mother answered, "We're from Germany, and we are going back soon." Kay looked around and said, "We sure do have a special neighborhood with people from all over the world."

"Yes," said Anna. "I'm from Puerto Rico."

Stevie looked up from petting Teddy and said, "We're from Brazil."

One little boy looked at Teddy and then pulled on his mother's shirt, "What am I, Mommy?"

She said, "Well, I'm from the Philippines, and your daddy is from Canada. I guess we are just plain people!"

Kay looked at the little boy and smiled. "We are all neighbors. Maybe you are like Teddy. Josh and I call him an ELF. That means an

'Especially Loved Friend' with a big heart. We aren't sure about just what kind of dog he is, but we know that he is smart, cute, friendly, and happy. I believe that he is going to become a very good friend and will help many people. Those are the important things to know about someone."

"Teddy is my friend, and I don't care what kind of dog he is," said Josh.

"Good-bye, ELF dog!" said Jessica, as she rolled away on her skateboard.

Teddy just lay in the sunshine on the grass and wagged his tail.

KAREN SPRUILL

# Teddy's Talking Time Questions for People

1. What parts of you have changed as you have grown and gotten older?

2. From what countries of the world did your family once belong?

**Write your answers below.
Draw how your pet has grown on the next page.**

# Teddy Tales

# 3

## Teddy and the Tummy Ache

*Sometimes, puppies and children put things
into their bodies that make them sick!*

Teddy is a puppy that likes to chew on everything he can find. He chews on his squeaky toys, and sticks in the yard, and leaves in the grass, and pieces of paper in the house. He chews on flowers, water bottles, and bugs. He also tries to chew on the towels, and the furniture and even people's shoes. He chews on peoples' fingers or clothes. If it is shiny or bumpy, or crinkly or lumpy, Teddy puts it into his mouth and chews it. And when he chews, he usually eats things.

Sometimes Kay sees Teddy chewing something and she cries, "No, No," and runs to open his mouth and get the object out before he can swallow it. She worries that someday he will eat something that will poison his body or hurt him in some way.

Kay wonders if Teddy is always hungry because he is growing so fast. She makes sure to give him lots of good things to eat and chew. He has puppy food with vitamins several times each day, clean water in his bowl, and dog treats. He also has peanut butter inside a special chew toy, and chew toys to eat that are shaped like bones. All of those things help him grow and become a healthy dog. Kay wants Teddy to live a long time so that she will have him for a friend and so that he can help special people with his love.

Since Teddy is really just a baby dog, people often say that he is "teething" or getting new teeth and that makes him want to chew things. Kay says, "Maybe his gums hurt or itch? Or maybe he is just very curious and learns about objects with his mouth." But Teddy certainly does get into a lot of trouble because he puts everything into his mouth. And some things are just not supposed to go into the mouth or into a stomach.

One day while Kay was talking on her telephone, Teddy was walking around the swimming pool. He liked to chew on the pretty plants and watch butterflies or birds fly by. This time he picked up some little white stones and chewed on them. When they didn't taste very good he just swallowed them anyway. Later he had his nap, a walk, his supper, and playtime before going to sleep in his dog crate bedroom.

Very early the next morning, Teddy woke up with a strange feeling in his stomach. He barked very loud, and then he barked again. Kay woke up and hurried to take him outside. Teddy was sick to his stomach all morning and couldn't eat his breakfast or drink his water. Kay knew that something was wrong with her puppy and that he needed to see the veterinarian. So early that day, Teddy got a ride in the car to see Dr. Henderson. Teddy stayed at the doctor's office for several hours so that they could take some pictures of the inside of his body, and give him some medicine.

Then the doctor called Kay, "You can come get Teddy and take him home. But I have some interesting pictures to show you first." When she returned to get Teddy, Dr. Henderson showed her the pictures of Teddy's stomach. Inside Teddy, there were two white stones that were the reason that he was feeling so sick. Stones do not belong inside puppies! The doctor reminded Kay that there are many things that puppies should not eat and that certain garden plants, and chocolate candy can also make a dog very sick.

Teddy seemed very happy to see Kay and he was in a rush to leave the office and get into the car. When he got home his smelled all his toys and took a nap.

When Kay told her husband, Sam, what had happened to Teddy, he said, "Our Teddy is a 'Rock Hound'." Kay was very glad that Teddy would feel better after the stones had passed through his body and he would not need to have surgery. He slept a lot that day and didn't want to play. He ate a little of the special food from the doctor and took his medicine.

The next day Teddy felt much better. Kay felt happy just to see Teddy playing and eating again. When Josh came to their house after school that day, Kay told him all about Teddy and the white stones that had been in his tummy. Josh petted Teddy gently and said, "I'm so glad that Teddy is going to be O.K. One time I was like Teddy. When I was little I ate some berries off of a bush and my mom had to call Poison Control. Teddy and I both got better!"

Kay hugged Teddy and said, "I wish Teddy could tell the story of his tummy ache to lots of children and people. It is very important what we put inside our bodies and our minds!"

# Teddy's Talking Time Questions for People

1. *How do you decide what is good to eat?*

2. *What should you do if someone eats something that will make them sick?*

**Write your answers below.
Draw your pet's favorite food on the next page.**

## Teddy Tales

# Teddy Goes to School

*Learning the rules helps everyone*

Teddy had been living with Kay and Sam for only a few days when Kay decided that he needed to go school! Teddy was constantly getting into mischief. Teddy pulled the toilet paper off of the roll in the bathroom, he grabbed Sam's slippers, and he pulled towels off of racks and dug holes in the yard. Kay told Teddy, "No…no…no," many times each day and he didn't seem to understand. She was afraid that he would believe that he name was "No no." Kay had taken her other dogs to training classes so she knew that Teddy would be more fun to live with if he went to school.

Kay went to the pet store and saw the circle of chairs and the special area for dog training classes. She asked one of the store clerks, "How old does a puppy have to be to attend classes?" The woman told her Teddy needed to be eight weeks old, and he was eight weeks old! The first class was just for the owners, and then there were seven more classes with owners and the puppies. So Kay signed up Teddy for the Puppy Training Class starting the next week. It would be fun to see what kind of puppies came to class and how they would grow each week.

The next week Kay left Teddy to play with her husband, Sam, while she went to meet the other puppy owners at class. "Hi, I'm Lindsay," said the friendly teacher. Lindsay told everyone about the kinds of things that they would learn together. She asked them to practice using different tones of voice for praising, and correcting their dogs. She asked them to reward their puppies for looking at them when they said the puppies' names. She showed them safe toys for their puppies, and asked them to bring a pocket full of treats as rewards for their puppies. Each week she would give them assignments to work on at home so they would be ready for class. She answered questions and tried to help people with their puppy problems.

When it was time to take Teddy to his first class, Kay put on his leash and let him sit next to her in the car. He was very excited and barked on the way to the store. She talked very calmly to him, "Everything will be all right." Inside the store he looked at everyone and sniffed everywhere as they walked to the class area. As the other puppies came into the class, Teddy pulled hard on his leash and wanted to go play with them. He was very happy when Lindsay arrived with her dog, Jack, and told the owners that they could let the puppies lose to play inside a special fence. Puppy class started with recess! Teddy barked and wiggled and pounced on some of the other puppies. Finally he found one special puppy that wanted to wrestle with him and they played until Lindsay said, "Get your puppies and we'll start class." By then Teddy was tired and ready to sit near Kay again and learn.

The puppies started to learn the words, "Sit," how to walk on a leash, "Down," then "Stay," and "Give." Next they learned, "Come," and "Wait." Kay enjoyed teaching Teddy and she liked to show some of her friends the things that he was learning. Teddy, Kay, and Sam now had words that they all understood.

Each week, Lindsay smiled at Teddy and greeted him, "Teddy, you are getting so big!" When Teddy played with the other puppies, that made Lindsay laugh. Teddy loved going to school and play time was his favorite part of every class. Each week he could hardly wait to jump out of the car and run inside to see his friends.

Once on a rainy day, Kay took him to visit the pet store when it was not time for class. Teddy raced to the class area and looked for his friends but they were gone. He seemed rather disappointed when they walked through the aisles and looked at birds and fish. But he loved to see other dogs that were visiting the store with their owners. Sometimes he barked at them as if to say, "Do you want to play?"

Teddy soon learned more ways to obey his owners. It was getting easier for Kay to take Teddy on his walks and Teddy seemed to enjoy his homework. He liked to practice "Sit, down, sit," and he especially liked getting a yummy treat when he obeyed. He was very good when he started to eat something on the street and he heard the command, "Leave It!" Sometimes Kay thought that he started to eat something bad, spit it out, and then looked to see if she was ready to give him a treat. Sometimes it seemed like Teddy was training Kay. However, Kay knew she was a better owner for Teddy by going to classes with him.

One day while Kay was practicing with Teddy in the driveway, Josh arrived after school. "What are you doing?" he asked.

"We're practicing for Puppy Class. Teddy is learning commands and we have homework. It's kind of like going to school for dogs," said Kay. She asked Teddy to Sit and then Down, giving him a treat.

"Does he like going to class?" asked Josh. "Sometimes I don't like school."

"Teddy has important work to do when he grows up. He loves going to class to play with his puppy friends, and he likes his teacher. And the more that he learns about good manners, the more he can do to help people. When he's a little older we might go to Dog Obedience Class. Or we might even go to Agility Classes where he can have fun doing exercises and games. If he can become a Therapy Dog, we could take training from the Delta Society so we can visit schools and nursing homes," said Kay.

"Can I try?" asked Josh. Kay showed him how to ask Teddy to Sit and Stay and then release him to get his treat.

"If you ever get a puppy, remember to go to class together," said Kay.

On the last evening of class, Teddy and Kay had to pass a test where Kay would give Teddy some of the commands that they had learned together. They walked down some of the store aisles and Teddy obeyed commands. Lindsay said, "Good job, Teddy!" When they were done, Lindsay took their picture with Kay holding a little graduation hat over Teddy's head and she was given a certificate to take home. They had completed their Puppy Class. But it was just the beginning of more learning adventures for Teddy and Kay!

# Teddy's Talking Time Questions for People

1. *Why is going to dog training or to school important?*

2. *What are some commands that every dog should learn?*

**Write your answers below.**

# 5

## Teddy's Terrible Teeth

*Puppies' teeth and people's words can both bite!*

"Ouch!" cried Kay, holding her hand. "No Bite!"

Teddy, the puppy, was so excited about playing catch with his favorite toy that he bit into Kay's skin. "It's bleeding," said Kay, as she went to get a bandage. "I'm getting so tired of Teddy's biting." Teddy didn't understand why Kay or Sam did not want to keep playing when he chased their legs and they walked away. Teddy's teeth had also left little holes in some of Kay's jeans, shirts, and socks. Sometimes, Josh, the neighbor boy, went home after a visit with scratches on his hands or arms.

Teddy's puppy teeth were very sharp, and he loved to use his mouth on everything, including his people! Kay and Sam tried lots of ways to discourage him from biting. They said, "No!" or "Ouch!" in a very loud voice. Sometimes, they used a spray bottle of water to surprise him and squirt him, when he bit or barked too loud. Sometimes too, they sprayed one of his favorite chewing spots with a special water that tasted like bitter apples but would not hurt him. Other times, Kay just put him into his bedroom crate and let him calm down. Kay worried that Teddy might accidentally hurt Josh or another visitor with his sharp teeth. She had several small scars on her arm as a reminder of his rough playtimes.

Kay knew that puppies bite a lot when they play and that they learn about life by tasting and feeling things in their mouths. Teddy's gums might have been itchy or sore as he lost his puppy teeth and got ready for new teeth. She also knew that certain kinds of dogs are especially designed to bite and kill small animals, while other kinds of dogs have "soft mouths" that don't usually hurt things so much. Whatever was causing Teddy's problem, in order for all of them to live together, he had to learn what he could and could not bite.

Kay was glad when a few ideas seemed to help Teddy not to bite so much. She had learned that one of the best things to do with a dog with a rough mouth was to stop playing with him. She tried to make sure that Teddy had plenty of safe, chewy treats to gnaw on, besides sturdy toys to play with. After Teddy attended Puppy School, she was able to give him some commands such as "Sit" or "Down," and then he seemed to forget that he had been playing roughly. She and Josh practiced giving him commands, followed by treats when he obeyed.

Kay also liked to take him to the pet store or a dog park, where he could have play time with other dogs. Puppies have lots of energy and silliness, so they need exercise and play time. Kay learned that puppies need other dogs to help teach them manners about how hard they can bite. Teddy didn't bite as much, when he had other dogs to play with.

But Teddy had other problems with his mouth. Sometimes, Teddy used his loud bark when he dropped his toy and couldn't reach it. His bark was very sharp, and it hurt everyone's ears. "Sh-h-h-h," Kay would say to Teddy, or "Quiet."

## Teddy Tales

"I wish he could understand to use an 'indoor voice,'" Kay said to Josh.

One day, when Kay and Josh took Teddy out in the neighborhood for his afternoon walk, they saw some of the children playing in a yard. Teddy got excited, and his tail started to wag. Suddenly, Kay heard one of the bigger boys yelling at little Andrew. "Stupid," "ugly," and "dummy" were some of the words that the big boy was saying to the smaller boy. The older boy ran out of the yard as Kay and Josh walked by with Teddy.

Several children saw Teddy and ran to greet him. "Can we pet him?" they asked.

Kay pulled Teddy's leash closer to her and told Teddy to "Sit."

"Sometimes, he gets excited, and he nips, but he doesn't mean to hurt you—just be careful. We are trying to teach him manners," she said smiling. Lots of hands reached out to pet Teddy, and he tried to jump and lick them. "One at a time, please," said Kay.

"O-o-h, he bites," Andrew cried out, and he jerked his hand away. Kay saw tears in his eyes.

"Did Teddy hurt you?" she asked. Andrew searched his finger and shook his head, "No."

"Did that big boy hurt you, Andrew?" asked Kay.

"That's my brother," Andrew pouted. "He hurts my feelings, and I don't want to play with him."

"My baby sister bites, and I don't want to play with her," said Josh, as he stroked Teddy's back.

"Puppies and kids have to learn not to hurt their friends—or their brothers and sisters—with their mouths," Kay said. "Words can hurt just as much as a puppy's sharp teeth, can't they?" she asked. "If Teddy bites someone, we can't undo a scar. We can't take back words that bite, either."

Andrew smiled a little as Teddy calmed down and sat in the grass licking Kay's hand. "See, Teddy can learn to be kind and gentle with his mouth."

"I wish my brother would be kind and gentle. Then I could play with him," said Andrew.

"I have to let Teddy know when he hurts me. Maybe next time your brother calls you names, you could say, 'when you call me names, that hurts my feelings.'"

"No more biting words!" said Andrew, and suddenly he jumped up and started to run after his friends. "Thanks, Teddy."

"Let's go home, Teddy," said Kay. "We'll find you a new chewy bone and a snack for Josh."

Teddy Tales

# Teddy's Talking Time Questions for People

*1. What can help a puppy learn to not bite?*

*2. What can you do when a person uses biting words?*

**Write your answers below.**

# 6

## Teddy Makes Friends

*Friends can come in all sizes, shapes, and ages*

When Kay adopted Teddy, he was used to living with his eight brothers and sisters, and the other dogs waiting to be adopted at Buddies for Life. Every time Kay took him for a walk he looked around for dogs to play with. Oh, he liked to meet people but he especially yipped and cried whenever he saw a dog. "I have never had such a friendly dog before," said Kay. "He would like to have a dog party every day!"

Teddy wanted to rush right up to any dog he saw—big or small, young or old—Teddy wanted all of them for friends. Usually when the dogs met, they gave each other their special dog greeting by sniffing under each others' tails or between their legs. Then they might go around and around trying to chase each other. Kay would get a little worried if Teddy's new friend stopped wagging his tail, growled or had hair raised along its back. She did not want Teddy to get hurt and she wasn't sure that he understood all the dog signals for, "I don't want to play."

Teddy even wanted to be playmates with Tigger, Kay's old cat. And Sam and Kay tried to make sure that Teddy wouldn't hurt Tigger. However, Tigger did not want to be chased and licked so he hid under the bed and would not come out. "Poor Tigger, he doesn't want to have a puppy in the house," said Sam. Kay wished that the two pets could enjoy each other. Tigger had lived with their last dog and even learned he could step around her while the dog slept. But Kay knew that dogs and cats don't always make best friends. Finally they decided that Tigger should go to live with their son because Tigger just could not enjoy life with Teddy. "Not everyone wants to be friends, Teddy," Kay said as they waved good-bye to Tigger.

About six weeks after Teddy came to live with Sam and Kay, their daughter came to visit them. She brought along her dog, Silky, a Borzoi, or Russian Wolfhound. Kay wondered how the two dogs would get along in the house. When Lilly and Silky arrived, they gave Teddy a new toy and something to chew. Teddy was so happy to meet Silky that he wanted to play with her all the time. Sometimes she just lay down and seemed tired of his nipping and wrestling. But they also went on walks together while Kay and Lilly talked. On the day that Silky had to get in her car to go home, Teddy stood in the driveway and barked and cried as though he wanted to go with her. He sounded like his little dog heart was breaking.

One day when Kay was in the back yard with Teddy, her neighbor, Jim, looked over the fence and noticed that she had a new dog. "Hey, what a cute puppy. Where did you get him?" he asked. Then he picked up Teddy and showed him to his own dog, Duke. Now Duke was a big gray Weimaraner. But Teddy was not afraid of him. "Duke is gentle," said Jim. And he put Teddy down where the two dogs could meet. Instantly Duke and Teddy started playing together—chasing and wrestling on the grass. They played until Teddy was panting and his pink tongue hung out of his mouth.

Soon after that whenever Teddy was in the yard and heard the neighbor's door open, or could hear Duke's backyard chain rattle, he cried to see Duke and jumped up on his fence. Several times each week they played together. Jim told Kay about a fun park where dogs could run free and play together. So one weekend, Sam and Kay took Teddy in the car and drove to the nice park by a river. They kept Teddy on a long leash so he wouldn't get lost or hurt. He enjoyed the trails and then he saw some dogs playing together. He ran to meet the big black dog who seemed friendly. Sam laughed and took some pictures of Teddy and the big dog. The dog's owner said that Samson was only nine months old. Teddy was only four months old. But Teddy did not seem to notice that Samson was a Great Dane. He wrestled and rolled and chased with the big dog until Samson went to play with a couple of other big dogs.

Not long after that Jim told Kay that they would be moving. They let Duke and Teddy play together as often as possible until moving day. Kay was sad for Teddy that he would lose his best friend. For several days after they had gone away, Teddy ran to Duke's driveway and sniffed, looking for him. Kay was glad that Teddy still had friends to play with at Puppy Class and at the dog boarding kennel. And she knew that Teddy would always be trying to make new friends.

When Kay learned that some of their friends were also getting a rescue dog, she was happy for them. Fred and Sara had chosen to adopt a rescue Greyhound named Dina. Dina used to work at a racetrack but now she was going to be a companion for Fred. Kay called to see if she and Teddy could visit Dina and welcome her.

Teddy was happy to get a car ride and he was excited to see Dina. But Dina wasn't sure if she liked Teddy and she backed up and stayed near Fred's legs. Finally Fred put Dina inside their house while he and Kay talked about dogs. Then Kay and Teddy went home. "I'm not sure if Dina wants to play with you Teddy," said Kay. She decided that they would visit another time after Dina has a chance to feel more at home.

For awhile Kay could tell that Teddy missed his old friend. He had lots of toys at home, and several walks each day but he seemed to get bored. He always had fun when Josh, the neighbor boy, came to spend some time after school. Josh rolled a ball for Teddy to fetch, and Josh helped Teddy go outside so he wouldn't have accidents on the rug.

One day Kay was glad when one of her friends called and said that she gotten a new puppy. Not long after that Susan called, "Can Otis come over and meet Teddy and play?"

"That would be great! They can play together on the kitchen floor. And we have some puppy toys that Teddy has outgrown that Otis can take home," said Kay. When Otis came to the house, Kay could see how much Teddy had grown. Otis was an eight-week-old West Highland Terrier puppy and Teddy was a lot bigger than him. Otis seemed sleepy, but Teddy just barked at him until he started to wrestle. Kay and Susan watched to make sure that no one got hurt while the puppies played. Teddy had another new friend! The next time that Otis came to play he didn't let Teddy rest.

## Teddy Tales

When Teddy goes on walks around his neighborhood he meets little Chihuahuas, Beagles, Basset Hounds, Dachshunds, a Poodle, a Scottish Terrier, a Boston Terrier, Labrador Retrievers, and Afghan Hounds. Most of the dogs and their owners are friendly and will stop to say hello and see if the dogs like each other. Sometimes they keep right on walking. Sometimes the other dogs growl or don't want to play.

Sometimes Teddy and Kay meet a strange dog that is loose without an owner and that makes Kay worry. Teddy is still a puppy and they could both get hurt. So Kay carries a special whistle with her in case of danger and sometimes she takes along a stick. When she meets a loose dog she keeps Teddy very close to her and stays as far as possible away from the other dog or they quickly walk back toward their own house. It's not safe for dogs to be loose in the neighborhood without their owners. They could get hit by a car or bitten if they got into a dog fight.

Kay is trying to set up a play date with a neighborhood puppy. She has also seen dog play groups listed in the newspaper so there are other ways for Teddy to keep making friends. They plan to visit some dog parks where dogs can run free and play together without their leashes. Teddy doesn't care about the size or color or age of the other dogs. Kay tells her friends: "Teddy is a positive dog. He acts as though every dog will be fun to play with and he gives every dog a chance to become his good friend!"

KAREN SPRUILL

# Teddy's Talking Time Questions for People

1. *How can you tell if a dog or cat is not friendly?*

2. *Does it matter if your friends don't look like you, or they are older or younger, bigger or smaller than you? Can differences be a good thing?*

**Write your answers below.
Draw your pet's friendly face on the next page.**

# Teddy Tales

# 7

## Teddy's Big Sleepover

*Learning to sleep away from home can be fun*

Sam and Kay were going on vacation and they could not take Teddy along. So Kay started to think of who could take care of Teddy while they were away from home. Puppies cannot be left alone for long periods of time, nor can they be shut up in their kennels for hours. Puppies need lots of exercise, and naps, and someone to make sure that they don't hurt themselves. Caring for a puppy takes a lot of time and patience.

Kay asked one of her neighbors who always liked dogs if she could take care of Teddy, but Pat said, "I am afraid that Teddy is getting too big and strong for me to handle him." Then Kay thought about Josh, who came to her house several times a week after school, but he was in school every day. Teddy would need someone to play with him many times during the day.

Then Kay called phone numbers of some people who just visit dogs in their houses to care for them but that seemed very expensive and Teddy would still be alone too much. Then she called some businesses that just let dogs play and live at their building while their owners are at work or gone away. One place said, "Sorry, we don't take puppies until they are six months old." Finally Kay decided that Teddy would stay at Miss Carrie's where he had once gone to play with dogs during the daytime.

While Kay was busy packing her own suitcases, she packed things for Teddy's big sleepover also. He would be at Miss Carrie's for 12 nights. So she measured out his dog food into little plastic baggies for each day, and she packed some dog biscuits—one for each day. And she wrote a special note and sent along his flea medicine pill. Then she collected his favorite blanket, and several of his stuffed animal toys to put where he would sleep. She knew that sometimes it helps to have some things that smell like home, food that you are used to, and a favorite toy when you have to sleep somewhere new.

Kay knew that she would miss Teddy while she was on vacation. She loved his cute little face and playing with him. She knew that he would grow some more while she was gone away. She did not want him to become sad and feel like he had been given away. She did not want him to cry at night. She hoped that he would remember her when she got back! She wanted him to stay healthy and eat his food and have fun.

So on the morning of the day that they were to leave for vacation, Kay put Teddy's special overnight bag into the car, spread a blanket on the back seat, and went to get Teddy. He loved to ride in the car and he was very excited. Then he settled down on the backseat and took a little nap while Kay drove to Miss Carrie's.

When they arrived, Teddy couldn't wait to run inside and see some of his dog friends. Kay gave his bag of belongings to a young woman who took them to another room. Then she took Teddy and Kay patted Teddy and said, "Good-bye." The woman at the desk asked if there were special instructions for feeding Teddy. She reminded

Kay that they could call at any time and see how Teddy was enjoying his stay. As Kay walked away from the building, Teddy jumped onto the fence in the yard and Kay said good-bye again and felt sad. Maybe Teddy was a little scared about her walking away.

Kay felt better when she remembered that the people who took care of the dogs loved them very much and that they treated them with much kindness. The dogs went outside sometimes, and they also got to play with other dogs. Teddy would have food and water each day, and be put into his own kennel each night. Someone stayed all night to watch over the dogs.

Of course, Sam and Kay didn't forget about Teddy. The very first day while they were on vacation, they went into a little pet store and bought Teddy a new toy. Sam showed the shop owner a picture of Teddy and they talked about dogs. They had a good time seeing new things, and eating good food, and visiting with their daughter, but every few days they would remember Teddy and looked forward to seeing him again.

Late one evening Sam and Kay finally returned home from their vacation. They wanted to go get Teddy and bring him home but they knew that he would be so excited that none of them would get to sleep that night. So early the next morning they both decided to bring Teddy home again. Sam had to go back to work but he didn't want to miss getting happy puppy kisses and giving Teddy a big hug. Traffic was slow and they could hardly wait, but finally they drove up to Miss Carrie's and went inside.

When one of the women brought Teddy out to them, he wiggled and jumped with delight. "Wow, he grew while we were gone," said Kay. Teddy's legs looked longer and his fur appeared longer and grayer. One of the helpers, said, "Oh, we will miss you Teddy." Then he started barking at Sam and Kay, just like he was telling them something important. After paying for Teddy's sleepover, Sam and Kay and Teddy raced to the car and drove home. Teddy seemed like he was in a rush to go back home.

Back inside his house, Teddy sniffed his food and water bowls, and then he sniffed all of his collection of toys and pulled out one of his favorites. "Welcome home, Teddy," said Kay. "You were a brave puppy and I'm proud of you." Then Kay took him on a walk around the neighborhood and he seemed very happy to see and smell everything. "It's good to go away, and it's good to come home," said Kay as Teddy settled down in his favorite spot for a nap. Kay was sure that there would be more vacations and more sleepovers for Teddy and that he would be all right.

TEDDY TALES

# Teddy's Talking Time Questions for People

1. *Teddy could not stay overnight at some places because he was too young. How old do you think someone should be to go on a sleepover?*

2. *What are some important things to remember to take for a sleepover?*

**Write your answers below.**

# 8

## Teddy—Curious and Cautious

*Paying attention with our senses brings surprises*

Teddy uses all of his doggie senses. He is very curious. He listens for voices and for knocks on the front door. When a person sneezes, his ears perk up and he will walk up to their face and sniff. He knows the sound of the garage door each evening when Sam comes home. He hears dogs barking inside their houses when he walks by on the sidewalk. He loves the taste of peanut butter, the feel of a good belly rub, or soft tissue paper in his mouth. He always notices the smell of meat, and the sound of his favorite squeaky toy. He enjoys watching the neighbor mow her lawn from inside the front window of his house.

One day Teddy kept putting his head under one of the couches at home. He would whine and bark. Kay looked and could not see any lost toys or bits of dog treats. Finally, she pulled out the couch and a big dead insect was lying next to the wall. After she threw it away, Teddy stopped barking. "I guess your nose smelled that bug," said Kay. "I'm glad you notice when things change. You can help warn me of dangers. And you will be a great detective!"

On another day when Josh was visiting at their house, Teddy began barking at the swimming pool. Josh looked up from his homework and said, "I'll go see what he wants." He came back in and opened his hand for Kay. "Oh, where did you get that?" Kay jumped at the sight of a little dead frog. "Teddy found it floating in the pool," said Josh, as he put the frog into the trash. "Teddy has a gift for noticing things," said Kay.

Teddy also noticed very loud noises. When he was a little puppy, he seemed to enjoy everything. However, as he grew up, he started to learn that some things could hurt. During the Fourth of July celebrations, Teddy learned about the sound of fireworks. He pricked up his ears, and then surprised Sam by jumping into his lap – all 40 pounds of Teddy. When he heard his first thunderstorm, he spent about 30 minutes on Kay's lap, breathing very fast. "Maybe the sound hurts his ears," she said. "We'll just try to stay very calm." Kay knew that when someone is afraid, it only makes them feel worse if the people around them talk loud and move fast. She talked very quietly to Teddy, hoping that he would breathe more slowly, and then she scratched behind his ears, and gently moved him to the floor.

Kay and Sam started to notice that at times when the television was turned on, Teddy began to howl. After a while they realized that during one certain commercial, Teddy would cock his head when he heard the announcer's voice, and as soon as the song started, he would howl like a wolf. "Music is not the same to dogs as with us," said Kay. "There must be some notes in that song that he doesn't like or mean something special in dog language." So they tried to silence that commercial whenever it started to appear.

While repair people came to the house to fix some windows, Teddy watched them from inside. Kay talked softly to him, "It's OK,

Teddy," and tried to help him understand that she knew about the men--that they were allowed in the yard. However, for several days after the men left, Teddy did not want to go out of the door into the yard where the men had worked. He had a good memory and he was getting very cautious.

As Teddy got older and the time for Halloween grew closer, he started acting a little more scared on his walks. One day they walked by a lawn that had a scarecrow in the front and Teddy did not want to go near that thing. He stopped and Kay had to talk gently and pull on the leash to get him to move. She touched the scarecrow and showed him that it was not alive. "Some things look real, but they aren't, Teddy," said Kay. Another day, they saw a person in a costume walking down the street and Teddy stopped to stare at him. "Teddy, you notice everything," said Kay.

A little further, down the street, the Webster family had an inflatable pumpkin in their yard. When Teddy saw the wind blowing the strange new object, he jumped straight up and twirled with his leash. Some kids in the next driveway started to laugh. "He's spooked by Halloween," said Michael. Another time when some neighbors spoke to Teddy, he jumped back. "Teddy, you are a scaredy-cat!" said Jill. Kay did not like having someone call Teddy a name just because he was afraid. Calling names does not help when someone is afraid. Besides, everybody feels afraid sometimes!

When Sam and Kay had guests at Christmastime, Teddy was afraid of several of the new people in his house. "Teddy, come here," they said and reached out their hands to him but he backed away and barked. Usually Teddy jumps with joy to greet visitors that he knows. So everyone laughed. "I'm sorry," Kay told the guests, "Teddy will need more time to learn to trust you. You know, sometimes it is not a good idea to go to strangers, even if they call your name!" Later in the evening, Teddy got braver when he could see that the visitors were safe people.

Now Kay likes to tell her friends about Teddy's special curiosity and his funny cautious ways. One day when Teddy was outside on the back porch, Kay heard him bark very loud. She thought that was his signal to come inside so she went to open the sliding door. However, Teddy did not want to come in. He was standing and watching a big bird high in the sky over the backyard. When Kay looked up, she could see the white head and wide wings of an American Bald Eagle circling their home. Kay smiled and patted Teddy's head, "You found your first eagle, Teddy. I might have missed that. Thanks for sharing it with me." After that sometimes she called him, "Eagle-Eye Ted"-- A puppy that notices many things and who is always curious and cautious.

# Teddy's Talking Time Questions for People

1. *What might help when someone is afraid?*

2. *What is the difference between being cautious and being afraid?*

   **Write your answers below.**

# 9

## Teddy and the Haircut

*A new haircut requires love and patience*

Teddy the rescue puppy turned two years old, and his owner, Kay said, "Teddy is like a teenage dog now—almost all grown up." Teddy was bigger and heavier than when he was a puppy. Sometimes he forgot he was big and he still jumped into Sam's lap and licked Sam's face. Kay took a picture of them with her camera because they looked so funny.

Since Teddy was a rescue dog, no one knew for sure what he would look like when he grew up. Kay thought it was a nice surprise that Teddy's kind of hair did not shed and get all over the floors and furniture. But Teddy's hair had a special way of collecting everything that it touched. Kay called it, "Velcro® fur." Teddy's hair collected leaves, sticks, fuzz, dust, string, and little burs from the grass. After a walk, Kay would often spend many minutes pulling little burs or stick-tights out of Teddy's feet and legs.

One of the ways that Kay knew Teddy was becoming all grown up was because of the change in his hair. Teddy's hair had gotten grayer, thicker and much longer. The hair on his paws grew until Kay said his feet looked like "dust mops." The hair on top of Teddy's nose and between his eyes had to be trimmed or else it would fall in front of his eyes. The hair on his ears was getting longer and his beard was getting long, his tail was getting long—he was becoming very hairy all over. Everywhere that Teddy went where children saw him, they usually shouted, "Hey, it's the Shaggy Dog!" Even Josh, the neighbor boy who came to Kay's house each week starting calling Teddy, "Shaggy."

Kay had a special dog brush that she had used on Teddy since he was a puppy. Now she needed some other kinds of brushes. So she went to the store and found a "pin" brush that had lots of little metal pins to help get through lots of hair. And she bought a de-matting comb so that she could work through some of the snarls in his coat. Another time she bought a special kind of brush with batteries inside the handle. That brush was supposed to help keep dog hair from smelling stinky. Teddy never really liked the electric brush since it made a little clicking noise.

Kay and Teddy had a routine each day when she brushed Teddy. She wanted his coat to look soft and smooth, and keep it from getting snarled into tight clumps or mats. Also, she liked it when they went on walks and neighbors said, "Oh, what a pretty dog." Sometimes in the morning when Teddy first came out of his bedroom crate, Kay said, "He looks like a big gray rug." And then he laid on the floor and let her brush him all over his body. When Kay brushed around his ears and head, he was let out a big "Sigh-h-h-," as if he was really enjoying his brushing. She brushed one side and then the other side saying, "Over," half way through and Teddy would get up and lay on his other side. When Kay found snarls behind his ears or under his front legs, she would get the de-matting comb or sometimes she had to get a small pair of scissors and cut out the clumps. Usually Teddy was very patient to become all brushed and fluffy. Sometimes he got a treat for being such a good dog.

Every couple of months, Teddy's long hair started to smell very strange. Then Kay knew it was time to give Teddy a bath. Since Teddy was a little puppy, Kay gave Teddy his baths in a big metal tub near the back door. She would fill up the tub with warm water, and make sure to have several buckets of rinse water nearby. Then she would lift him into the tub, tell him to "Sit and stay," get his fur all wet, put on doggie shampoo and scrub him clean. He seemed to like getting a bath and usually did not try to run away. But he looked like a very different dog when his fluffy hair was all wet. "You are mostly fur," Kay said to a wet, skinny Teddy. Then she would lift him out, and rub him all over with a towel. Teddy would shake the wetness out of his fur, all over Kay, and then try to find a place to rub his wet face. Kay would not let him outside in the yard until she had dried him for a while with her hair dryer. She had to work fast because he did not like the noisy hair dryer. When he was all done, he would run very fast around the back yard. Kay would be very tired from all the work.

One day Sam offered to give Teddy his bath in the shower. Sam got in first and he and Kay coaxed Teddy into the shower stall. Kay held the door shut since Teddy wanted to escape. Sam picked Teddy up and got him all wet, and then he put dog shampoo on his fur and rubbed it in. He rinsed him off with a little bucket and finally told him to "shake." After he shook off some of the water, they let him out of the shower and Teddy tried to rub his face on the bathroom rug. Kay quickly rubbed him with a towel, and then used the hair dryer, being careful not to get the heat too close to his body. When he was almost dry, Kay combed out his hair.

During the summertime, Kay decided that Teddy might be more comfortable if he got a haircut. "It will grow back in the winter, and I won't have to brush his hair so much," she said to Sam. So Kay made an appointment with a dog groomer, a woman who washed and clipped dogs at her home. Now Teddy had had baths away from home before when he went for boarding. But this was his first big hair cut. Kay tried to tell the groomer what she wanted Teddy's hair to look like, and then she put him in a waiting kennel and went home for a while. Nan, the groomer, said, "I'll call you when he's done and you can come get him." Teddy barked as Kay left without him.

When Kay came back to pick up Teddy, she was very surprised. All over his back the hair was quite short, and a little longer on the sides. His beard and ears looked very different. The hair above his eyes was trimmed. His paws looked smaller. He looked like a new dog! He smelled like special perfume and he had a kerchief tied around his neck. He was very happy to see Kay and rushed to get into the car. Kay paid the groomer and took Teddy home. Kay wasn't sure if she liked this new haircut or not.

When Sam saw Teddy that night, he said, "Wow. Who is that dog?" Then he played with Teddy and petted his back. "Oh, he's very soft," said Sam. He looked at Kay and told her, "It's still Teddy. The hair will grow back." They took him on a walk and tried to get used to Teddy's new look. "Just think how much easier it will be to take care of him," Sam reminded Kay.

## Teddy Tales

The next day, Josh came to stay with Kay for awhile. When he first walked in and saw Teddy, he started to laugh. "Look at us," he said when he petted Teddy. Kay looked at Josh and saw that he had a new summer hair cut also. "Teddy is not Shaggy anymore, and neither am I!" said Josh. "Did he cry last night?"

"No, but I almost did when I first saw him," laughed Kay.

"I did not like my hair yesterday. When I came home my little sister called me, 'Baldy'. And when I went to bed I felt sad and started to cry."

"Oh, short isn't bad, and it's very soft on top," said Kay, rubbing Josh's head. "It's just different. The hair will grow back!" Teddy jumped up and licked Josh's face.

"We are the same boys underneath," said Josh.

KAREN SPRUILL

# Teddy's Talking Time Questions for People

1. How do you know when you need to take a bath or shower?

2. What can help if you get a "bad" haircut?

**Write your answers below.
Draw your pet at bath time on the next page.**

# Teddy Tales

# 10

## Teddy the Runaway

*Sometimes we want to run away when a loved one is sick*

By the time that Teddy, the rescue dog, turned three years old, he and Josh, the neighbor boy, had spent lots of time together at Kay and Sam's house. Every Tuesday and Thursday, Josh came after school to do his homework and play a game until his parents got home from work. Kay was very fond of Josh and Teddy, and she called them, "her boys." Josh was also one of Teddy's special people. Josh said, "Teddy has a 'fav's list, even if he doesn't have his own phone." Teddy barked and jumped for joy whenever his favorite people came to visit.

One day when Josh was doing homework at Kay's kitchen table, he seemed especially sad. Teddy came and put his paws in Josh's lap. Kay looked up from her computer and said, "One of Teddy's gifts is having radar for when people are hurting or sad. I call him my 'comfort dog.' Are you sad today?"

Josh shrugged his shoulders and said, "Maybe."

Kay sat down beside Josh and handed Josh a ball of clay. Kay knew that boys sometimes use their hands to help them talk about feelings.

Josh gave a big sigh. "My grandpa is in the hospital. We went to see him this weekend and I was afraid," Josh slammed the clay onto the table. "Grandpa had tubes and a mask on his face. He didn't look the same. I couldn't hug him good-bye—I just ran out the door. He must think that I am a coward."

"Oh, Josh," said Kay. "I have a Teddy story to tell you."

"One time Sam got very sick and needed to stay home from work. Sam's stomach and head hurt and he stayed in bed all day. Teddy sniffed at Sam in the bed, and then I shut the door to the bedroom and told Teddy to 'stay out.' All day, Teddy had to stay out of the bedroom. That evening, I decided I wasn't going to disturb Sam, so I would sleep in the guest bedroom.

"When it was almost bedtime, Teddy wanted to go outside. I opened the sliding door to the backyard and let Teddy go out. After I put on my pajamas and brushed my teeth, I called Teddy to come in. But Teddy did not come. I turned on the backdoor light and called for Teddy. But Teddy did not come. It was getting late and I wanted to go to bed. I found a flashlight and put on my shoes. I walked around the backyard and called Teddy's name but I did not see my dog.

"Once I thought I heard Teddy bark. I got scared and wondered if Teddy had somehow run away. So I opened the yard gate and walked around the outside of the fence calling, 'Teddy, Teddy,' hoping that I wouldn't wake up the neighbors. My heart was beating fast and I was worried. What if I couldn't find Teddy?

"I decided to come back inside the backyard with my flashlight and carefully look under all the bushes. Under the biggest bushes, I saw two red eyes shining. Sure enough, it was Teddy. 'Teddy, you get out of there!' I scolded. He would not move. Finally, I got several of Teddy's favorite treats and came back to the bush. 'Teddy, come get TREATS,' I called. At last Teddy came out from under the bushes at 11 o'clock at night.

"The next day I told Sam about our runaway dog. Teddy seemed to know that Sam was not well. Maybe he was trying to run away from his scared feelings. But Sam got better and Teddy never ran and hid under the bushes again. Now he even likes to comfort me when I'm sad.

"So I am pretty sure that your Grandpa understands that you love him, even when he's sick and you are afraid. Sometimes as we grow up, the very things that frighten us turn into a strong point, with some time and courage. When Teddy was a puppy, we didn't know all of his gifts. While he has grown, he has shown us his strengths. Just like you, Josh. Your gifts are still growing. "

"I guess dogs and kids are a lot alike," said Josh. "Teddy and I both beg for treats too! Can we have a cookie now?"

# Teddy's Talking Time Questions for People

1. *Have you ever run away and why did you?*

2. *What is one of your gifts or special abilities?*

**Write your answers below.
Draw your pet's favorite hiding place on the next page.**

# Teddy Tales

# 11

## Teddy's Beach Vacation

*It's fun to go away and it's fun to return home*

One fall day, Kay and Sam's neighbor boy, Josh, came back to their house after school. That afternoon he brought in some shells he had found on his summer vacation at the beach. Kay admired the pretty shells and they talked about Josh's trip.

"Most of the time, I liked our vacation," said Josh. "But I didn't get to go with my dad on his fishing trip. And I hated sleeping in the same bed with my brother. My mom got really mad at me once in a restaurant when I made a mess with my spaghetti. And I got sunburned and it hurt."

Kay laughed, "Josh that sounds like our beach trips with Teddy. Remember several years ago when I told you that Teddy got to go to a dog beach the first time? The sand was very hot and hurt our feet, Teddy tried to drink the salt water, and on the way home he discovered he liked ice cream. Well, last weekend, Sam did some research and found a place that let dogs stay overnight with their owners for extra money. He wanted to try Teddy on an overnight trip to the beach."

"Wow, did you go swimming Teddy?" Josh patted Teddy's head and went to sit on the couch with Kay.

"First we stopped for a picnic on our way. Sam thought we could eat at a roadside park but when we were hungry and wanted to stop, a sign said No Dogs near the picnic tables. So I looked in the special dog book that our son and daughter-in-law gave us. We found a town with several parks where we could eat a picnic with Teddy on a leash. We found a park, walked Teddy and then he sat by the table while we ate. I took some of his treats and water bowl along, but his favorite part of the trip was riding in the car.

"The place where we stayed overnight had several other dogs with their owners. Sam took Teddy's crate along and set it up but Teddy was too worried to even go near it. He wanted to be with us all the time. We could not have left him in his crate or he would have barked and cried.

"After we got unpacked, we drove to a dog beach where most of the dogs run free. We found a dog that looked a lot like Teddy at that beach. Her owner said, 'I think your dog is a Bearded Collie!' Teddy actually went into the water and didn't seem bothered. He stayed very close to us. We tried to sit on a towel but lots of dogs kept running by us and kicking sand on us. Some of the dogs chased Frisbees® into the waves, some dogs dug big holes in the sand, and others just wanted to sniff the other dogs. Sam took lots of photos of the sunset and the dogs. When we got ready to leave, there was a special little doggie shower so you could wash the salt off of the dog. I toweled him off and we went back to our room."

"Yeah, my mom makes me take a shower after going in the ocean," said Josh. "What else did Teddy do on his trip?" asked Josh.

"We also ate together at a special restaurant that allows dogs on the patio. It was called *The Old Salty Dog*. Teddy sat next to us on his leash, and the waiter brought him a water bowl and some dog biscuits. He really liked the biscuits. People walked by him and kept talking to him. One lady came over and asked to pet him. He was quite the star of the evening. We thought the food was good too!

"The next day, we ordered some take-out food for breakfast and ate outside by our room. Teddy remembered the restaurant and he wanted some of our food. Then Sam and I took turns walking on the beach near our motel since that one doesn't allow dogs. Each of us took Teddy on a long walk while the other person was gone. Teddy was very anxious when one of us walked away. We had to keep him busy until we were all back together. Then Teddy watched while I took a swim in the pool. While I packed, Sam took the dog crate apart. When we got home we found out that he had forgot and left some of the parts at the motel.

"On our way home, we stopped at another dog park that we had found in our book. It was a large, shady park with lots of big dogs. One of them wasn't very nice to Teddy and his owner didn't make him behave, so we didn't stay very long. Teddy was happy to go back in the car and sit in the backseat. After a long ride, Teddy came home and had a long nap."

"Do you think Teddy will go on vacation with you again?

"Well, we all learned some things on our trip. Teddy was pretty easy to travel with since he was just glad to go with us. And he did not get car sick. Teddy learned that he didn't want to take his eyes off of us or get left behind! But most of all, I think we learned that you have to do your homework when you take your dog with you on vacation. Maybe more places would welcome dogs if their people would pay attention to them, clean up after them, and teach them traveling manners."

"I hope Teddy and I get to have more vacations—because mostly it is fun," said Josh. "Can we play a game now?"

## Teddy's Talking Time Questions for People

1. What kinds of things should you think about when taking a dog on vacation?

2. Why aren't dogs allowed on all beaches and parks?

**Write your answers below.
Draw your pet in his favorite place on the next page.**

# Teddy Tales

# 12

## Teddy's Dog Family

*Our hearts must remain open for all family members who are near and far, young and old, in all shapes and sizes*

"Kay will be back soon," said Sam to Teddy, the rescue dog. That morning when Sam let Teddy out of his crate, Teddy went into the bedroom, jumped on the bed but he didn't find Kay, so he laid down on the floor with his head on his paws.

During Teddy's fourth summer, Kay took a trip and she was away from home for more than a week. Sam could tell that Teddy missed her. Kay missed Teddy too but she had an important job. She was helping their daughter move. At the end of the week Lilly and Kay would drive Lilly's car on a trip to move to Florida. Teddy didn't know that he would have a big surprise. They would be bringing Lilly's dog, Silky.

Kay and Lilly and Silky had a long car ride back to Kay and Sam's house. Silky slept on the backseat for most of the long car ride. They stopped each day for several walks and gave Silky a chance to drink water and use the grass. As they got closer to Kay's house, Kay said, "I wonder if Teddy and Silky will remember each other." Teddy and Silky had met several years before when Teddy was still a puppy. Silky had come to visit them for a few days. This time, Silky would be staying at their house for several weeks before going to live nearby in a new house.

When Kay and Lilly stopped in the driveway, they let Silky out and they opened the front door. Teddy seemed surprised to see all of them and he rushed up to Silky with little barks and squeals, his tail making big thumps of happiness. "He greets Silky as if she is his mother and he is a little puppy," Kay said. Silky walked around the house and Teddy followed her everywhere. After Kay and Lilly took luggage and bags inside the house, they took the two dogs on a walk around the neighborhood. Teddy wanted to stay very close to Silky.

As the two dogs got to know each other, they found each others' food dishes. Silky really liked Teddy's food, and she often finished what was left in his dish. Soon Kay moved Teddy's dish to another room and tried to keep the door shut but Silky would sneak into the room whenever the door was left open. Teddy liked to eat Silky's food also, and play with her toys.

When Lilly started working at a new job, sometimes Kay took the dogs on walks with a leash in each of her hands. Both dogs used Teddy's fenced back yard and when everyone left the house, Teddy stayed in his crate while Silky slept on the floor nearby. On the weekends, Kay and Sam and Teddy took Lilly and Silky on long walks at their favorite dog parks.

One day, Josh, the neighbor boy came to stay with Kay after school. He petted both dogs and helped Kay take them on a walk. "I'm proud of Teddy," said Joshua. He and Silky are sharing very well—they share the sidewalk, the water dish, toys, and the floor for naps!" "Yes," said, Kay. "They are becoming family."

## Teddy Tales

After Silky moved into her new house, Teddy seemed to look around for her at his house. And when he went to visit at her house, he was excited to see her again. Soon after her move, Silky became sick and had to go to dog doctors and take medicine. She didn't want to play with Teddy and sometimes she growled at him or turned away from him when they were together. Lilly was very worried that Silky might not get better. No one could understand why she was sick or when she might get better. She was too sick to take walks with Teddy and Kay.

When Joshua heard about Silky, he felt sad. "I hope she will get well," he said. "I bet Teddy misses playing with her. That's the way I feel when I visit my grandpa."

"How is that?" asked Kay while she got Joshua a snack of fruit and crackers.

"I used to have fun with my grandpa but since he got sick, he doesn't want to go fishing or riding bikes. He just sits in his chair and sometimes he is grumpy."

"When our loved ones get older and sick, we need to be very patient with them," said Kay. "They still need us but sometimes they can no longer do what they used to do with us. We can be thankful for the fun times we had together and try to find other ways to enjoy each other—like a good snack or a quiet game."

"Yes, I'll try that next time I'm with Grandpa," said Joshua. "He might not mind playing a game of checkers with me."

Weeks went by, and one day, Lilly called Kay with some big news. "We have a new dog, and her name is Star. Can Teddy come to visit our dogs?" So Kay took Teddy in the car to see Silky and Star. Teddy rushed into the house and the new dog was very surprised to meet him. Star was a Borzoi, just like Silky. She was mostly white with a few black spots on her long coat, and she was very tall and thin.

Star and Teddy jumped and ran and went in circles around the people, and furniture. Kay and Lilly laughed when Star would jump right over Teddy or he would walk beneath her tummy. Silky was feeling much better but she did not have as much energy as Teddy and Star. "Star is almost one year old but she is still full of mischief," said Lilly. "She likes to chew things, like the window blinds, and bags of dog food." The dogs went outside in the yard together and then played with some of Star's toys.

Later after Teddy went home, Lilly called Kay and told her that when Teddy left, Star had looked out the front door and howled and cried. "Star has a new friend and so does Teddy," said Kay.

Silky started to feel better and soon all three dogs were able to go on walks together. Sometimes they met at the local dog park. If Teddy arrived before Silky and Star, Kay would say, "Your girls are coming, Teddy," and when he saw them arrive at the park, he would run to the gate and start barking. Sometimes Teddy and Star and some other dogs would race together. Then Star could run faster than any dog in the park.

## Teddy Tales

On Star's birthday, all the dogs went on a walk together and played in her house while the people watched a movie. Sometimes Star wanted to wrestle with Teddy and swat him with her long legs, then he would bark at her until she would stop. Sometimes they would both tug on the ends of a toy and growl at each other. Silky would slowly follow them or just watch them from her favorite resting place.

On New Year's Eve, Kay and Sam invited Lilly's family to come to their house, and of course, Silky and Star came along. Star and Teddy barked at each other and chased through the house. Star and Silky drank water from Teddy's bowl, visited the backyard, and later Kay gave all three dogs some special treats. While the people played card games, the dogs slept on the floor around the table.

When Lilly and the dogs went home, Kay said, "Thanks for coming to Teddy's New Year's Eve party. Our first annual dog party!" As Teddy watched out the front window, Sam patted his head and said, "Young and old, people and dogs—now Teddy really has a family."

Karen Spruill

# Teddy's Talking Time Questions for People

1. What kinds of things do you share when you are part of a family?

2. How can you help older family members when they are sick?

   **Write your answers below.**

CPSIA information can be obtained
at www.ICGtesting.com
Printed in the USA
FFOW03n0055301017
41641FF